Little Genie
Make a Wish!

Little Genie
Make a Wish!

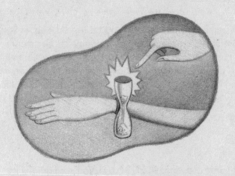

MIRANDA JONES

illustrated by David Calver

SCHOLASTIC INC.

New York Toronto London Auckland Sydney
Mexico City New Delhi Hong Kong Buenos Aires

ISBN-13: 978-0-439-89604-7
ISBN-10: 0-439-89604-5

12 11 10 9 8 7 6 5 4 3 2 1   6 7 8 9 10 11/0

Printed in the U.S.A.   40

First Scholastic printing, September 2006

Special thanks to Narinder Dhami

Don't miss these great books!

Little Genie

Make a Wish!

Double Trouble

And coming soon:

A Puff of Pink

Castle Magic

Contents

Chapter One
Nothing Ever Happens in Cocoa Beach

August 31

<u>How I Spent My Summer Vacation</u>

By Allison Katherine Miller

I bet you're wondering why I'm writing this. Fourth grade hasn't even started yet! I guess I have a lot of time on my hands. Oops! Not that much time. Gran'll be here soon to pick me up. So here it is.

<u>Summer highlights</u>

Staying up late ON WEEKNIGHTS!

Riding Splash Mountain with Mary and screaming like crazy!

Fishing with Dad

No homework! (That one's good enough to repeat. No homework!)

<u>Summer lowlifes</u> (Or is it low*lights*? In any case, they're low.)

Reruns

Mosquito bites

Listening to Jake twenty-four hours a day

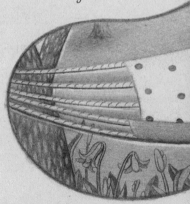

Now that I think about it, it wasn't a bad summer. But I wish something really exciting had happened. Something a little out of the ordinary. But nothing ever happens in Cocoa Beach.

Chapter Two
Saturday Treasure

"Ali Miller!" boomed a loud voice. "Stop right there!"

Ali nearly jumped out of her summer-tan skin. She spun around and saw a huge stone statue of a woman holding a vase. It sounded as if the voice had come from the statue itself. "Buy me now, Ali," the voice boomed again. "Pleeease take me home with you!"

"Oh, Gran!" Ali groaned as she suddenly recognized the speaker. She turned bright red when she saw that people were staring at her. "Everyone's looking!"

Ali's grandma popped her head out from behind the statue. "Isn't this great?" she said, a grin on her face. "Don't worry, I'm not going to buy her. She'd never fit in my car!"

Ali laughed. She called Gran the Junk Queen. Gran's house was full of old stuff she'd collected at garage sales and flea markets, just like the one they were at now. Although Ali didn't like it when her grandma did something embarrassing, like wearing that awful floppy hat or hiding behind statues, she really looked forward to their Saturday bargain-hunting trips.

Sometimes the things people didn't

want were really weird! And what was even weirder was that other people wanted to buy them! Today Gran had already bought a smelly one-eyed teddy bear, a cracked china teapot, and a carton of musty old books. "Saturday treasures," she called them.

Ali hadn't bought anything. She still had two dollars tucked inside her flower-shaped change purse. She'd been hoping to find some cool barrettes or maybe a poster of her favorite band, BoyFrenzy. So far, she'd had no luck.

Gran moved on to the next stall and started poking around in some cardboard boxes. Ali hurried after her. It was so hot! Maybe after this Gran would find a nice lemonade stand.

"Look at this, Ali!" Gran smiled. "Isn't it wonderful?"

Ali stared at the dusty, dirty object her gran was holding. It didn't look that wonderful to her.

"It's a Lava lamp," Gran explained.

"Well, it looks pretty ancient," Ali said. She'd seen Lava lamps at the mall. When the lamp heated up, the colored wax inside moved and stretched itself into fantastic shapes. But this lamp looked as if it had given up long ago. The wax looked hard as rock. The liquid surrounding it was a murky blue, and what had once been bright pink was now the color of old bubble gum.

"That's because it's an original model," Gran said, brushing off some of the dirt.

She peered at the bottom of the lamp. "I bet it's from the sixties."

That did sound pretty ancient. But Ali didn't want to point that out to Gran.

"And you know what?" Gran said, her blue eyes twinkling. "My first boyfriend gave me one exactly like this for my seventeenth birthday!"

Ali grinned. She loved looking at photos of her gran when she was a teenager, with her black eye makeup, miniskirts, and big hair. Suddenly the dirty old lamp seemed much more interesting.

"Who was your first boyfriend, Gran?" Ali asked. She couldn't picture her with anyone but Gramps. And Gramps sure didn't look like a boyfriend.

"Oh, I had so many, I can't remember!"

Gran winked at Ali. "Actually, it was Eddie Norris, who lived next door to us."

"What happened to your lamp, Gran?" Ali wondered out loud. Then she gasped. "Maybe this is the very same one Eddie Norris gave you all those years ago!"

"No, it can't be." Gran shook her head. "My lamp got broken when your mother decided to play soccer in the living room."

Ali stared at the lamp and then felt for her flower change purse. It would be great to have something from the sixties that reminded her of Gran. And if she cleaned it up, it would look really cool. She could put it on the desk in her bedroom.

Gran saw the look on Ali's face.

"Would you like it, love?" she asked.

Ali's face lit up. "Oh yes, please, Gran!"

Gran beckoned to the man who was working in the stall. "Excuse me," she said, holding up the lamp. "How much do you want for this?"

The man looked surprised. "That old lamp? It doesn't work, you know."

Ali felt a bit disappointed. She'd been looking forward to trying the lamp out when she got home.

"But it's an original," the man went on hastily. "A bargain at six bucks."

Gran raised an eyebrow at him. "Three?" she said very sweetly.

The man thought it over. "Okay, three."

"Then we'll take it," said Gran. She whipped out her purse. "Don't worry, love," she said to Ali. "Your mom might be able to fix it."

Gran was always bringing her flea-market treasures over to the Millers' house and asking Ali's mom to make them work.

"Or Jake might be able to break it," Ali pointed out. There was no way she was letting her little brother—otherwise known as Bulldozer—touch the lamp.

Gran handed the man three dollar bills. "You know I'm no good at fixing things," she went on, wrapping up the cord and giving the lamp to Ali. "Did I ever tell you about the time I took my grandfather clock apart? When I put it all back together again, the hands went backward instead of forward!"

Ali took the lamp and stroked the cold, dusty glass with her hand. She really hoped her mom would be able to get it to work. A Lava lamp that didn't light up wasn't nearly as cool as one that did.

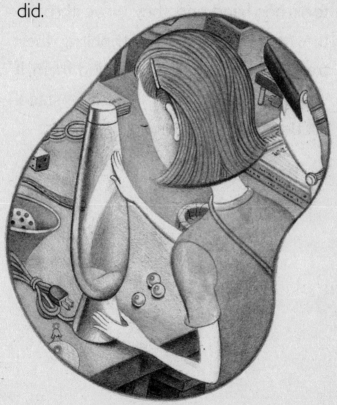

Then again, it had only cost three dollars. "You get what you pay for," Gramps was always saying.

"Looks like you're my Saturday treasure," Ali said to the lamp as Gran took her hand and they wove through the crowded flea market, pulling their treasures in a metal cart behind them. If only they could find a lemonade stand, Ali decided, things would be perfect.

Chapter Three
A Puff of Pink

"Gran, this one-eyed teddy bear smells disgusting," Ali grumbled as they pulled into her driveway. She took her Lava lamp out of Gran's carton of books, which was next to her on the backseat.

"He'll be fine after he's had a good scrub-a-dub," Gran promised, turning around in the driver's seat.

The front door opened and Ali's mom came out. "Hi," she called as Ali got out of the car. "More junk, I see!"

"They're interesting objects, dear, not junk!" Gran scolded out the window. "Don't fill my granddaughter's head with that poppycock."

Ali leaned forward and gave her a kiss. "Bye, Gran. Thanks for the lamp. And for the lemonade and the funnel cake," she whispered.

Gran kissed her back. "Ali's got a surprise for you," she told Ali's mom. "Bye." She waved and sped off down the street.

"Hmmm, let me guess," Mom said. "Doll clothes with missing buttons? Some old board games in dented boxes? Or is it a watch without a battery?"

"A Lava lamp," Ali replied, holding it up in the sunshine.

"Hmmm." Mom frowned at the dusty

object. "Does it work?" She followed Ali inside.

"Um, not at the moment," Ali admitted. "Gran said you might be able to fix it." She smiled hopefully. "You're so good at that kind of thing."

Mom laughed. "You two are as bad as each other with your junk!" she teased. "I'll have a look at it later. I've got some papers to go through, and then we'll have lunch before the boys get home. Okay?" Ali's mom worked in a bank. Sometimes she brought work home on weekends.

Ali nodded. That meant she had time to clean up the lamp before her mom looked at it. She went into the kitchen and found a dust cloth and some cleaning spray.

Just as she was about to head upstairs to her bedroom, the phone rang. Ali picked it up. "Hello?"

There was a burst of noise at the other end. Then a familiar voice shouted, "Hi, Ali, it's me!"

"I know!" Ali laughed into her best friend Mary's ear. "I can hear your dad!"

Mary's dad tried to keep up with the music Ali and Mary listened to. He was always belting out the latest song from BoyFrenzy. The trouble was, Mr. Connolly's singing voice sounded like a strangled sea lion, and he didn't know any of the songs' real words, so he just made them up as he went along. Mary thought he was very embarrassing. Ali thought he was funny.

"Hey, Dad! Give it a rest! I'm on the phone!" Mary yelled. "Can you believe school starts next week?" she asked Ali.

Monday was the start of a new school year at Montgomery Elementary School. "I know! I'm so glad we're in the same class again." Ali sighed. "I hope we like Mrs. Jasmine."

"Have you got your notebooks and stuff?" Mary asked.

"Not yet," Ali said. Getting new supplies was the best part of going back to school. "Gran bought me this really old Lava lamp today." She squinted at the glass. "It doesn't work, but my mom's going to fix it for me."

"Cool," Mary said. "Maybe I can come over tomorrow and see it."

There was the muffled sound of Daniel, Mary's thirteen-year-old brother, shouting in the background. "You're not the only person who needs to use the phone, you know!"

Mary and Daniel were always arguing. Daniel was tall, noisy, and dorky. Ali's mom said it was because he was thirteen. Luckily, by the time Jake turned thirteen, Ali would be doing something very grown-up and sophisticated.

"Sorry, Ali," Mary said, sounding exasperated. "I'd better go before Daniel explodes. See you tomorrow!"

Ali clicked off and ran upstairs. She put the lamp carefully on her desk. She tucked her light brown hair behind her ears and studied the lamp for a moment.

Then she sprayed some cleaner on the dust cloth and started to wipe away the dirt.

"Ick!" Ali said as little flecks of grime rained down on her floor. The dust on the lamp was so thick it left grubby smears at first, so Ali rubbed harder.

Suddenly she stopped. The glass felt warm underneath the dust cloth, and a faint pink glow was coming from the lamp. It grew stronger and stronger. Small pink blobs of wax began to float dreamily around in the pale turquoise liquid.

Wow! Ali thought. *It does work!* The man at the flea market had been wrong. "I bet he'd be mad we only paid three dollars," she said to herself.

Fascinated, she stood back and

watched as more pink bubbles of wax floated upward. Then she frowned. "Wait a minute," she said out loud. "I didn't plug it in. Did I?"

Ali grabbed the lamp. When she held it up, the plug dangled in midair. She froze, clutching the lamp tightly. If she hadn't plugged it in, how was it working?

One of the pink wax bubbles caught

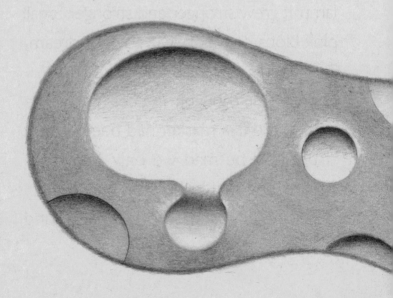

Ali's eye. As she watched, the bubble stretched and twisted, and twisted and stretched, until it didn't look like a bubble at all. And the liquid became bluer and brighter. Ali peered through the glass, straining to see. She blinked. Then she blinked again.

The bubble had grown arms and legs. And now it was growing a little head, topped with a bobbing ponytail.

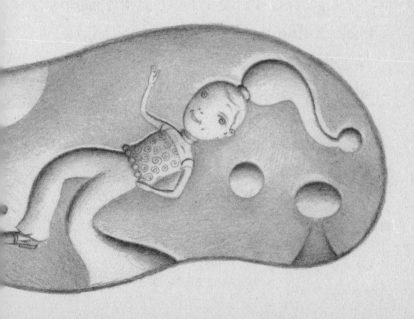

There was a tiny girl in the lamp!

She swam gracefully among all the pink bubbles, swooping and diving inside the glass tube. She was wearing wide brightly colored pants, a tight-fitting top, and golden slippers with curled-up toes.

Ali's heart thumped crazily. She was seeing things. She *had* to be seeing things.

Then the tiny girl waved to her.

Ali gasped and quickly put the lamp back on the desk. A puff of pink smoke swirled around the lamp, hiding it from view. The smoke made Ali cough, and her eyes watered.

"Hi, Ali," called a high-pitched voice. "We meet at last!"

Rubbing her eyes, Ali spun around.

Who was that? There was no one else in the room!

"Down here!" the voice called.

It was coming from Ali's desk. As she looked down, the smoke began to clear.

Waving and smiling up at her was the girl from the lamp!

Chapter Four
Snap Your Fingers

"Groovy!" The tiny girl danced up and down on the edge of the desk. "I can't believe I finally got out of that lamp after all these years. What a drag!"

Ali stared. Was this really happening?

The tiny girl smiled. "Hey, don't flip your wig. Just snap your fingers."

Ali stared some more.

"If you snap your fingers, I'll be full size,

just like you!" Then the tiny girl frowned. "You do know how to snap your fingers, don't you?"

Ali gave herself a shake. Feeling so excited she could hardly breathe, she nodded.

Snap!

Instantly the room was filled with a cloud of pink smoke, brighter this time. Ali coughed and spluttered again.

"Out of sight!" The tiny girl—who was now a regular, full-sized girl—waved her hands as the smoke began to fade away. "Ah, much better," she said, stretching her arms over her head. "I haven't been able to do that in years."

"How—how long have you been in there?" Ali asked. She sat down on her bed with a thump. Okay, there was a girl in her lamp. Okay, the girl from the lamp was now standing in the middle of her bedroom floor. Okay, she was crazy.

"About forty years, give or take a few," the girl said sheepishly. "I was never very good at transformation magic. That's what comes of missing so many lessons at Genie School. But now that you've made me grow once, I'll be able to do it myself."

Ali stared. The girl grinned at her. "Little Genie, at your service," she said. "Well, not so little now! But I am quite small for a genie, you know. My friend Genius the Genie is over ten feet tall."

Ali's mind whirled. Had the girl really said *genie*?

"I'm very pleased to meet you," Little Genie went on. She bent over in a low bow. As she did, her long blond ponytail got caught in the curved toe of one of her slippers. "Ow!"

Ali shook her head and closed her eyes. "This must be a dream," she whispered. "You're not here, and I can't see you."

"Of course you can't," Little Genie said, sounding puzzled. "Are you playing with a full deck? You've got your eyes closed."

Ali opened her eyes. "Are you *really* a genie?" she breathed.

"Well, of course," Little Genie replied. "And you freed me from the lamp, so now I belong to you. That makes me your humble servant. Do you think I should call you Lord and Master?" She looked doubtfully at Ali.

"I don't know," Ali said, surprised. "I've never met a genie before." She glanced over at the Lava lamp. "That doesn't look like the kind of lamp a genie would live in," she pointed out.

"Hey!" Little Genie sounded hurt. "That lamp was the coolest thing ever when I first moved in, back in 1964."

"So that's why you talk like that," Ali said, giggling.

Little Genie frowned. "Like what?"

"Never mind," Ali said. Who cared what this girl sounded like? She was a genie!

"It was a real bummer that I couldn't

get out for so long," Little Genie mumbled, looking down at her curly-toed slippers. "Honestly, genie lessons were so boring, Ali. Sorry. Lord and Master," she corrected herself.

"Just call me Ali," said Ali. "But why were the lessons boring? Don't you like doing magic?"

"Oh yes, I do!" Genie nodded so hard, her ponytail bounced up and down. "But before they let us do magic, we had to take classes like How to Keep Your Lamp Clean and Math for Modern Genies."

Ali couldn't imagine fitting a vacuum in a Lava lamp! And math wasn't one of her favorite subjects either. Maybe genies had problems with the same sort of stuff humans did.

"But you got to learn magic too, didn't you?" Ali wanted to know.

"Sure." Little Genie nodded. "But the teachers wouldn't let anyone do magic on their own to begin with. And I was stoked to try out my spells."

"So what did you do?" Ali asked curiously.

Little Genie looked very embarrassed. "Well, when the Grand Genie came to visit, I decided to give everyone a surprise and clean the school." Her ponytail sagged. "I did a spell and got all the brooms and dusters working on their own."

"What happened next?" said Ali.

"I couldn't stop them," Little Genie replied glumly. "There was soapy water and furniture polish everywhere. The floor was so slippery, the Grand Genie fell over!"

Ali giggled. "Did you get in trouble?"

"Well, it wasn't exactly the first time I'd gotten a spell wrong, so the teachers expelled me from school." Little Genie sighed. "Everyone else got to start doing magic, but I wasn't allowed to. One of the teachers, Miss Spelling, was nice to me, and she let me choose the Lava lamp to live in. I was supposed to stay in there and learn about magic, to make up for the missed lessons."

Little Genie stared at Ali, her eyes sad. "I've been in there for *ages,* because I had to wait for the eleventh owner of the lamp to release me." She brightened up. "And that's you, O Mighty Lord and

Master—I mean, Ali." She bowed, holding her head sideways so that her ponytail didn't get caught on her slipper.

"That bowing and stuff—is that all part of what genies do?" Ali asked. "It doesn't look very comfortable."

"Of course!" said Little Genie, looking surprised. "We learned that in Traditional Manners. I didn't miss *all* my lessons, you

know. Now, what do you want for your first wish?"

"My first wish?" Ali repeated.

"Are you thicker than a five-dollar malt? *Your first wish,*" Little Genie said slowly. "Don't you know anything about genies? You know, three wishes and all that?"

Ali didn't know what to say. Maybe she *was* thicker than a five-dollar malt. "Are you sure you weren't expelled before Traditional Manners?" she said finally.

She watched as Little Genie's pink cheeks pinkened even more. "Scratch that. Let me start over. O Lord and Master, for you I will capture the stars and harness the winds from the four corners of the earth. Your wish is my command." She bowed. "How did that sound?"

"Um, great," Ali said. "So, can I have my first wish right now?" Even though she still wasn't sure this was really happening, excitement bubbled inside her like cream soda.

Little Genie beamed. She gave a little dance of delight. "Yes indeed! Go right ahead. Oh, this is so exciting. After all those years, I finally get to do my first wish! Quick, think of something!"

This was the biggest moment of Ali's nine-year-old life, and she couldn't think of a single thing. She and Mary had sometimes talked about the things they would wish for. But right now, Ali's mind had gone totally blank.

Then, out of the corner of her eye, she noticed one of her magazines lying open on her pillow. She could see an advertisement for Tiger Chocolate, with a cute purple-striped cartoon tiger sitting on a chocolate bar.

"I want a tiger," Ali blurted out. "That's my wish." If Little Genie could make that wish come true, Ali told herself, then she would really and truly believe that she had her very own genie.

Little Genie raised her eyebrows. "Are you sure?" she asked skeptically. Her ponytail whizzed up and formed a question mark. "A real tiger?"

"Sure I'm sure." Ali grabbed the magazine and held the picture up. "Oh, maybe you don't have tigers where you come from. You *do* know what a tiger is, don't you, Genie?"

"Of course I do!" Genie looked hurt for a moment. Then she frowned, screwing her whole face up with concentration. She took a deep breath and snapped her fingers.

More smoke filled the room. It was lilac-colored this time, and even thicker than before. Ali began to cough. She could hear Genie coughing too. Smoke billowed all around them in great clouds, and Ali couldn't see a thing.

But she could hear something.

A loud roar, ringing around the room.

It was the roar of a wild animal.

A tiger.

Chapter Five
Wish Rules

"Help!" Little Genie wailed, clutching wildly at Ali. "It's a tiger!"

"I know!" Ali gasped. What had she done? She couldn't keep a real live tiger in her bedroom. Would it try to eat her? And what on earth would her mom say? "You're the genie—do something!"

The lilac smoke was beginning to drift away. Ali and Little Genie backed into a corner, still clinging to each other.

"What's that noise?" Ali whispered.

"It's my teeth chattering!" Little Genie whispered back.

They both jumped as another loud roar echoed round the room.

"Can't you get rid of it?" Ali asked desperately. An idea popped into her head, and she turned to Genie. "I want another wish," she said firmly. "My second wish is to get rid of that tiger!"

"It's not as simple as that." Little Genie let go of Ali as the last puff of smoke disappeared. "Look!"

Ali braced herself for a huge orange tiger with black stripes, ferocious eyes, and sharp teeth.

She blinked hard. There, sitting on her bedside rug, was a tiny, lilac-striped tiger.

He was no bigger than a kitten, and his fur was thick and fluffy. He stared curiously at Ali and Genie; then he opened his mouth and let out another earsplitting roar. Ali couldn't help wondering how such a little thing could make so much noise! But she couldn't possibly be scared of him.

"It's the tiger from the chocolate-bar advertisement," Little Genie said, beaming with relief. She pointed to the magazine on Ali's pillow. There was now a blank tiger shape in the chocolate ad. "My spell worked on the first try! He's cute, isn't he?"

"Well, he's certainly not what I expected." Ali smiled. But this proved it. Little Genie was the real thing!

Ali and Genie went over to the little purple tiger. He jumped to his feet and stood with his head cocked to one side, watching them.

"Good boy," Genie said as she bent down and patted the tiger. Ali did the same. It was like stroking a very soft kitten.

The tiger looked delighted. He rubbed his furry head against their hands, just like a kitten, and licked their fingers with his pink tongue.

"Well, your first wish didn't turn out too badly, did it, Ali?" said Little Genie, looking very pleased with herself.

"He *is* gorgeous," Ali admitted. The tiger was rolling over on the rug to have his lilac tummy tickled. "But I don't think my mom will let me keep him. She wouldn't even let me bring the school hamster home during vacation." She sighed. "I still think my second wish has got to be to make the tiger disappear."

"Oh no." Little Genie shook her head, her ponytail bobbing madly. "I can't do that."

"Why not?" Ali asked, surprised. "You said I could have three wishes."

"Yes, but there are wish rules," Little Genie said firmly, folding her arms.

"What rules?" Ali demanded.

"You can't unwish any of your wishes. So you can't wish the tiger away again."

Then Little Genie pointed to her wrist. She wore a gold watch in the shape of an hourglass. It was filled with sparkling pink sand.

"See the sand running through the hourglass?" Little Genie asked.

Ali peered at the watch. Sure enough, the pink sand was trickling through the hourglass very, very slowly, one grain at a time.

"You get three wishes in the time the sand takes to travel through the hour-glass," Little Genie explained. "And what-ever you wish for lasts for the same amount of time."

"How long will that be?" Ali gasped as she watched a single glistening grain of sand fall to the bottom of the hourglass. At this rate, the tiger was going to be here forever!

"Who knows?" Little Genie replied breezily. "Genie hours can last for days or even weeks. You can never tell how long they're going to be."

"That's just great," Ali muttered. It looked as if having wishes was going to be more complicated than she'd thought!

"That's magic, actually," Little Genie corrected her.

"Is there anything else I should know?" Ali asked, frowning.

"You can't tell anyone about me," Little Genie replied. "And I mean *anyone*." She shivered, looking scared. "If you do, I'll lose all my powers and be shut up in the lamp forever."

"Not even my best friend?" Ali asked, thinking of Mary.

"Nope."

Ali bit her lip. There was no way she

wanted Little Genie to lose all her powers and be a prisoner in the lamp. "Don't worry, I won't tell anyone," she promised. She stared at the tiger, which was padding around her bedroom, sniffing the furniture. He seemed quite happy exploring his new home. It looked as if he was there to stay—for a while, anyway. And he *was* very cute. She'd just have to try to keep him hidden from her mom.

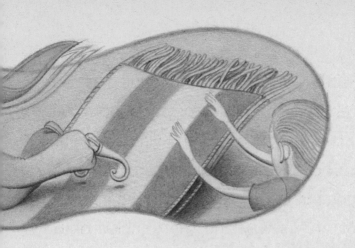

"At least he's being quiet now," Ali said.

The tiger bounded into the middle of the room and gave another enormous roar.

"Um, maybe not," Ali said, wincing.

"He might be telling us he's hungry," Little Genie suggested.

"Well, he could do it a bit more quietly!" Ali stage-whispered. Then she gasped as she heard footsteps on the stairs. "Oh no! My mom's coming! Quick! Grab the tiger!"

Little Genie lunged and missed as the tiger bounced off across the room. Ali rushed after him too and almost caught him, her fingers brushing against his furry body, but at the last moment he jumped out of Ali's way, and she tumbled onto the bed. The tiger shot off and hid under the desk, where he peeped out at them, purring happily. He clearly thought this was a great game.

"Here, boy!" Little Genie called, bending down and waggling her fingers at him. "Good tiger!"

The tiger looked up at them, his eyes bright with mischief and his tail swishing from side to side. He dashed out from under the desk and headed for the door. This time Little Genie was ready for him.

She threw herself full-length on the floor like a goalkeeper and grabbed him.

"Let's hide him in my bed!" Ali puffed.

Quickly they lifted the duvet and slipped the tiny tiger underneath. The tiger seemed quite pleased to have found such a soft, warm bed. He snuggled down quietly, curling his lilac tail around him.

"Thank goodness!" Little Genie sighed.

"But what about you?" Ali squeaked. Her mom was right outside the door!

"What?" Genie looked puzzled.

Hide! Ali mouthed at her as the door handle began to turn.

"Oh yes! Sorry!" And Little Genie vanished with a faint *pop.*

"Ali, what on earth is all that noise?" Mom said.

"What noise?" Ali asked, looking as innocent as she could.

"All that roaring." Her mom came into the room and looked around. "You must have heard it."

"Oh, *that* noise," Ali said, thinking fast. "It was probably Mrs. Carter watching TV next door. You know how much she likes those animal shows." She tried hard not to look at the small lump under the duvet.

"Well, let's hope she changes the channel," Mom said, shaking her head. "It sounded as if there was a wild animal in here!"

Ali smiled weakly as her mom went

out. She sat down on the bed, her knees wobbly with relief.

"Well, we got away with that, didn't we?" Little Genie piped up, reappearing on the bed right next to her.

Ali jumped. "Only just!" she said, wondering how long she could fool her mom. And Bulldozer—what would *he* do if he saw Little Genie? She didn't even want to think about it.

Ali pulled back the duvet and lifted the sleepy tiger onto her lap. "We'll have to find somewhere for him to sleep tonight, Genie."

Little Genie glanced around. "What about in here?" she suggested, bouncing across the room toward Ali's dresser. She opened the top drawer and grinned at Ali.

"This is perfect!" She pulled out a handful of Ali's socks. "The tiger will be snug as a bug in a rug in here."

"Let's see if he likes it," Ali said. She scooped the tiger up and carried him over, placing him gently inside.

"He'll feel at home with all those striped socks!" Little Genie laughed.

With a tiny purr, the tiger curled up on a pile of socks, tucking his paws neatly under his chin. When Ali reached out to

stroke his head, he nibbled gently on her fingers.

"Do you think he's hungry?" Ali asked, feeling worried. If the tiger was staying for a while, she wanted to look after him properly.

"Probably," Genie agreed. "Maybe we'd better feed him."

"I'm not sure what magic tigers eat," Ali said doubtfully. "But I'll go and see what we've got."

She hurried downstairs. Luckily, her mom was on the phone, so Ali was able to rummage in the fridge without having to answer any awkward questions.

"I wonder if he'll like this," Ali muttered as she picked up a plate of leftover lasagna. Looking after the tiger was almost like having her own pet, she thought with a grin. It was too bad she couldn't show him to anybody.

"I've got lasagna, bread and butter, lettuce, and ham," Ali announced as she entered her bedroom with a full plate. "Oh, and some cheese."

Genie was sitting on the bed with the tiger on her lap, tickling his chin. "Let's try the ham first," she suggested.

Ali held out a tiny piece to the little tiger. He sniffed at it, his whiskers twitching. Then he licked it with his pink tongue. He opened his mouth as if he was going to take an enormous bite, but then his head drooped and he turned away. He also refused the lasagna, the bread, and the lettuce.

When Ali offered him the cheese, he let out a mournful roar and hid under the duvet, leaving just his tail sticking out.

"He doesn't like any of it," Ali said, dismayed. "What are we going to do, Genie?"

"We'll just have to keep trying," Genie replied. "There must be *something* he likes. And we have to find out, because he could be here for quite a while."

They both stared at the hourglass on Genie's wrist. Hardly any sand had trickled through at all. Ali couldn't help feeling worried about her tiny new pet. Was she really going to be able to keep him hidden from her family until the hourglass ran out?

Chapter Six
Lots of Meows

"What's that?" Ali muttered sleepily. She was lying in bed, and something was tickling her nose. She opened her eyes. Morning sunshine was streaming in through the bedroom windows. The purple tiger was sitting on her pillow, swishing his tail from side to side and purring loudly.

"Isn't he sweet?" Little Genie's head popped out of the open sock drawer.

She had shrunk down to lamp size again and was wearing a pair of bright pink pajamas.

"What are you doing in there?" Ali yawned. "I thought you slept in your lamp."

"I do." Little Genie hooked one of Ali's long striped socks around the drawer knob, grabbed it, and swung herself down to the ground. She snapped her fingers and immediately shot up to full size. "But I heard the tiger whimpering in the night, so I got into the sock drawer to keep him company. I think he was a bit lonely."

"He seems all right now," Ali said, tickling the tiger's soft little ears. He started chewing on a corner of Ali's pillow.

"Hey, don't do that!" Ali scolded. The pillowcase was printed with pictures of BoyFrenzy. She tugged it gently from the tiger's mouth. "You can't eat that."

The tiger jumped off Ali's bed, landing neatly on all four paws. He let out a roar.

Ali clapped her hands over her ears. "We have to keep him quiet," she said as the tiger bounced over to Genie and rubbed his head against her ankles. "Bulldozer's probably watching cartoons, so he won't hear us, but my parents like to sleep in on Sunday mornings." She thought for a moment. "Maybe we should take him outside."

Little Genie looked thrilled. "That's a fab idea, Ali!" she cried. "Come on, what are we waiting for? Let's get ready!" She twirled around, her ponytail flying. There was a flash of blue smoke, and Genie's pajamas changed to sparkly blue pants and a matching halter.

Ali quickly pulled on a pair of shorts and a short-sleeved shirt and slipped on her sandals. Then she picked up the tiger and tucked him under one arm. He wriggled a bit but calmed down when Ali stroked him.

"You'll have to make yourself tiny," she reminded Little Genie. "Or the neighbors will get a big surprise!"

"You could say I'm a friend who's staying with you," Genie suggested, twirling her ponytail.

"No way," Ali said firmly. "What if they

ask my parents about you? How will I explain *that*?"

Genie nodded and snapped her fingers. With a faint *whoosh,* she quickly shrank until she was lamp size again, about as tall as a pencil.

Ali picked her up and put her in her shirt pocket. "Shhh." She put a finger to her lips as she opened the bedroom door. No sign of Bulldozer. "Don't make a sound."

"Okay," said Little Genie, wriggling farther down in Ali's pocket. Then she gave a yelp. "Ow!"

"Quiet!" Ali shushed.

"Sorry, I got my hair caught on a button," Little Genie whispered.

Hardly daring to breathe, Ali crept past

her parents' bedroom door. She tiptoed downstairs, trying to stop the tiger from wriggling out from under her arm. He was sniffing the air and getting very excited.

As quietly as she could, she crept past the hallway that led to the den. She could hear crazy cartoon laughing coming from inside.

Ali heaved a sigh of relief as they reached the kitchen. She unlocked the back door and went into the yard. A large white fence encircled the property.

Little Genie popped her head out of Ali's pocket. "Ooh, look!" she shouted, pointing at the stone birdbath in the middle of the lawn. "A swimming pool!"

Ali bent down and let Little Genie

climb out of her pocket and onto the edge of the birdbath. Luckily her dad kept it very clean. Genie rolled up the legs of her silk pants and began splashing her toes in the water. Ali put the tiger down on the grass and watched him race off into the bushes, his little paws a purple blur.

"Hello, Ali," called a voice from the other side of the fence.

"Oh no!" Ali gasped. She hadn't noticed their next-door neighbor, Mrs. Carter, hanging out her washing on the clothesline. Genie was still splashing around in the birdbath, singing to herself. Ali hoped Mrs. Carter couldn't hear her.

"Hello, Mrs. Carter," she called back, trying to sound normal. "How's

Marmalade?" Marmalade was Mrs. Carter's ginger cat. He was very beautiful, with bright gold and orange stripes, but he was the most timid cat Ali had ever met. Sometimes he even seemed to be scared of his own shadow!

"He's fine," replied Mrs. Carter, pinning a towel to the line. "At least, he would be if the other cats didn't keep bullying him!"

Ali nodded. She'd often seen Marmalade being chased around his own yard by the neighbors' cats.

"Poor Marmalade's stuck in the house," Mrs. Carter went on. "I think he's too scared to come outside. I don't know *what* I'm going to do."

A loud purring sound made Ali jump.

The tiger! She'd almost forgotten. He was rolling about on the grass, enjoying the sunshine. Luckily, Mrs. Carter was too busy with her washing to notice him. She was trying to hang a big white sheet on the line, but the breeze kept flapping it in her face and wrapping it round her legs.

"Ali, look at me," called Genie. She'd climbed down from the birdbath and was sitting in the sunshine. She had a large yellow-and-white daisy on her head. "Do you like my sun hat?"

"It's lovely!" Ali laughed. Then she turned pink as Mrs. Carter looked curiously at her. "Um, I was just thinking about a joke my friend Mary told me," Ali explained quickly.

"Oh?" Mrs. Carter looked interested.

"Why don't you tell it to me?"

Ali's mind went blank. She couldn't remember any jokes at all. "Sorry," she mumbled. "I can't remember it exactly."

Then her eyes almost popped out of her head. A yellow-and-white daisy was hurrying across the lawn toward her!

"Genie!" Ali breathed. To her horror, Mrs. Carter chose that very moment to

look over the fence into the Millers' yard.

The flower stopped and froze. Ali held her breath and looked at Mrs. Carter. Had she spotted Genie underneath the daisy?

"That's a pretty flower," said Mrs. Carter. "But it's growing right in the middle of your lawn. Your dad will have to be careful when he mows the grass."

Ali gave a sigh of relief. "Oh yes, I'll tell him," she said.

As Mrs. Carter started struggling with her sheets again, Ali rushed over to Genie. "What are you doing?" she whispered. "Mrs. Carter nearly saw you! I don't think I could have explained a daisy that can walk!"

"Sorry!" Little Genie grinned up at her.

"But I had to get to you somehow. It's the tiger!"

"What about him?" Ali looked at the spot where the tiger had been a moment ago. Now there was no sign of him. "Oh no, where's he gone?"

"Look!" Little Genie squeaked, pointing across the lawn.

Ali spun around just in time to see the tiger disappear through a gap in the fence—right into Mrs. Carter's yard!

"Oh no!" she gasped, racing over to the fence. Ali had used the gap before when she went to visit Mrs. Carter and Marmalade. Maybe she would have time to grab the tiger before Mrs. Carter spotted him. At the moment Mrs. Carter had her back to them, trying to peg another wet sheet to the line while the wind flapped it in all directions.

But Ali was too late. As she reached the fence, she saw the tiger race up to the cat flap in Mrs. Carter's back door. He poked the cat flap curiously with one paw, and it swung open. He pushed his striped head through and then jumped inside. The flap swung shut behind him.

Ali groaned. She turned around to find Genie next to her, still hiding under her daisy. "Genie," she whispered. "Do something!"

"Don't worry," said Genie. "Maybe our tiger will make friends with Marmalade."

"He'll scare Marmalade to death," Ali half shrieked. "And Mrs. Carter, too! Look, she's nearly finished hanging out her washing. We've got to get the tiger out of her house!"

"Leave it to me," Little Genie said confidently. She sat down cross-legged on the lawn, closed her eyes, and started whispering.

Ali waited impatiently. "Well?" she demanded when Little Genie opened her eyes.

"Hang loose," Genie said. "The tiger should be here any minute now. I did a summoning spell. I *think* I remembered the right words."

"Well, where is he, then?" Ali asked, looking around.

Just then there was a loud meow. And then another. A big black-and-white cat jumped onto Mrs. Carter's fence from the yard on the other side. Then a tabby cat appeared from behind the shed at the bottom of the garden, followed by a small white cat with bright green eyes. All three were yowling at the tops of their voices.

"Goodness me!" gasped Mrs. Carter as a fat ginger cat and a jet-black kitten joined the first one on top of the fence. She clapped her hands over her ears as all five cats wailed loudly. "Where have all these cats come from?"

"Genie!" Ali whispered, her heart racing. "What have you done?"

"Er—I suppose it *might* be because of my spell," Little Genie admitted, her cheeks turning red. She and Ali peered through the gap in the fence into Mrs. Carter's garden.

More cats were arriving from all over the place. Now there were eight cats sitting on the fence, their tails swinging. There were six cats sitting on the shed roof and another five milling around Mrs. Carter's legs. The noise was deafening as they howled and yowled.

"Shoo!" shouted Mrs. Carter, clapping her hands. "Go home, all of you!" But none of the cats took any notice. Mrs. Carter looked worried. "I'd better go inside and make sure Marmalade's all right," she said. "I'm sure all this noise must be scaring him."

"Maybe we ought to try to get rid of these cats first," Ali suggested quickly. She didn't want Mrs. Carter walking into her kitchen and coming face to face with the tiger!

"How on earth are we going to do that?" asked Mrs. Carter, a bewildered expression on her face.

"Yes, Genie," Ali whispered hotly to the daisy beside her. "How are we going to get rid of them? Can you do another spell? Quick, before they wake my parents up!"

But before Genie could say anything, Ali noticed that the cat flap in Mrs. Carter's back door was beginning to open ... and a lilac-striped head popped out!

Chapter Seven
Strong Little Paws

Ali's heart sank. She glanced at Mrs. Carter. Luckily she was still trying to shoo the cats away and hadn't noticed the tiger.

Ali leaned over the fence and waved to the tiger. "Come here, boy," she called softly. "Come to Ali!"

Suddenly the tiger opened his mouth and let out the most enormous roar! The cats in the yard almost leapt out of their furry skins. With loud yowls, they took off in all directions, their tails down and their ears flat against their heads. They looked terrified!

"Go, tiger!" Genie yelled, jumping up and down.

"Shhh!" Ali said.

Mrs. Carter clutched her chest as a sea of cats swarmed past her. "What was that noise?" she cried. "It came from my house!"

She spun around and stared at the cat flap. Ali and Genie looked too, and they both breathed a huge sigh of relief. The tiger had vanished back inside. Now Marmalade was peering through the cat flap, his green eyes huge with surprise.

"Marmalade!" Mrs. Carter exclaimed,

beaming with pride. "Did *you* scare all those cats away? I didn't know you could roar so loudly."

"Neither did Marmalade!" Ali whispered to Little Genie, trying not to giggle.

"I told you our tiger would make friends with Marmalade," Genie whispered to Ali.

"I'm not surprised," Mrs. Carter went on as she pinned the last sheet to the line. She smiled. "I always knew Marmalade could be brave if he wanted to be."

Suddenly the big black-and-white cat jumped onto the fence again. He glared at Marmalade, who quickly disappeared into the house. Ali watched, holding her breath. A second later, a familiar purple head popped through the cat flap. The tiger let out another earsplitting roar, and the black-and-white cat fled with a startled yowl. Ali couldn't help laughing when she saw that the tiger was gone again, and Marmalade's ginger head was sticking out through the cat flap by the time Mrs. Carter turned around.

"Well done, Marmalade!" Mrs. Carter said, picking up her empty washing basket. "I don't think we'll be bothered with all those cats coming into our yard again," she said happily, heading back to the house.

"Ali, the tiger!" Little Genie whispered urgently from underneath the daisy. "He's still in the house!"

"Let me open the door for you, Mrs. Carter," Ali said quickly. She squeezed through the gap in the fence and rushed over. She *had* to get to the kitchen and grab the tiger before Mrs. Carter spotted him!

Ali pushed open the door and glanced around the kitchen. Marmalade was hiding under the kitchen table, his ginger fur fluffed up in alarm. But where was the tiger?

Then Ali saw a flash of purple out of the corner of her eye. The tiger was chasing Marmalade's toy mouse around the kitchen. Quickly Ali scooped him up and pushed him under her shirt just as Mrs. Carter stepped into the room after her.

"Thank you, Ali," Mrs. Carter said gratefully. She put the basket on the table and bent to pick up Marmalade. "Who's a clever boy, then?" she cooed proudly, tickling the ginger cat's chin.

Marmalade let out a feeble mew and

snuggled into his owner's arms.

"I'd better be going," Ali said, turning away before her neighbor could spot the lump under her shirt. The tiger's soft fur tickled her skin.

"Oh, stay and have some lemonade," Mrs. Carter invited. "I'm just going to make a fresh pitcher. And I've got chocolate chip cookies too. I know they're your favorite."

Ali hesitated. She *loved* chocolate. It was her absolute favorite food. But she couldn't eat a chocolate chip cookie and keep hold of a wriggling tiger at the same time!

"No, thanks, Mrs. Carter," she mumbled. "I'm not very hungry."

"All right." Mrs. Carter looked concerned. "But that's not like you, Ali. Are you feeling all right?"

"I'm fine," Ali said weakly, backing toward the door. She was holding on to the tiger through her shirt with both hands, but she was afraid he was going to escape at any moment. He was squirming and prodding her stomach with his strong little paws. She was even more afraid that he was going to let out another roar and give the game away! "My mom's probably wondering where I am. Bye!"

Chapter Eight
Disappearing Chocolate

"Genie!" Ali whispered as she squeezed back through the gap in the fence. "Genie, I've got him! Little Genie? Where are you?"

There was no answer. The daisy was lying on the ground, and Little Genie was nowhere to be seen. Where could she be? Hoping it was somewhere safe, Ali hurried indoors with the tiger. Her mom was in the shower, and a note said

Dad and Jake had gone to pick up doughnuts for breakfast, so she rushed upstairs to her bedroom, opened the sock drawer, and popped the tiger inside. He seemed quite happy to be back. He yawned, showing his tiny white teeth, and curled up on a pair of Ali's wooly socks.

Ali looked in the lamp and under her bed, but there was no sign of Genie. She hadn't had any breakfast yet, and the doughnut shop was a good way away. Maybe she'd have some chocolate from the secret supply under her bed.

Ali pulled her special chocolate tin out from under her bed, opened it, and peered inside. It was empty.

"That's weird," she said to herself. "I'm sure there were two candy bars in here yesterday." She looked around her bedroom in case she had taken them out and forgotten them, but she didn't see them anywhere.

All that talk about chocolate chip cookies had made Ali hungry. She knew there were some cookies in the cookie jar, so she ran downstairs. But when she looked inside, the jar was empty. All that was left were a few crumbs.

"Darn," Ali muttered, annoyed. "And where's Little Genie gone?"

"Who are you talking to, Ali?" asked her mom, coming into the kitchen.

"Oh! N-no one," Ali stammered. "Just clearing my throat."

"Oh, Ali!" said her mom, spotting the empty cookie jar. "You've eaten all the cookies?"

"No, I haven't," Ali protested, but Mom still looked mad.

"Well, I'm not buying any more until I go shopping next week," she said sternly. "So you and Jake are going to have to wait." Shaking her head, she began to unload the dishwasher.

Feeling puzzled and a bit fed up, Ali grabbed an apple and went back upstairs. Why was all the chocolate in the house disappearing? And where was Genie?

"Oh, there you are!" Little Genie's head popped up out of the sock drawer as Ali walked into her bedroom. The tiger popped up beside her. "I've been looking everywhere for you."

"And I've been looking for *you*," Ali grumbled. "I barely got out of Mrs. Carter's house without her seeing the tiger. And now all my chocolate's vanished!"

Little Genie looked a bit sheepish. "Yes, I wanted to talk to you about that," she began.

"Ali?" Her mom was calling from the bottom of the stairs. "Mary's here."

"Oh! Time for me to disappear!" Little Genie patted the tiger and grinned at Ali. "Remember, don't say a word to your friend about me, okay?"

Ali nodded, wondering what Little Genie had to say about the chocolate.

But there wasn't any time. As Little Genie climbed out of the drawer and onto Ali's desk, something fluttered to the floor. Ali picked it up and stared at it. It was a candy bar wrapper from one of her candy bars!

"Genie!" she began, but just then there was a puff of pink smoke as Genie disappeared into her lamp. A second later, the door opened. Ali shot across the room and slammed the sock drawer shut, with the tiger inside it.

"Hi!" Mary grinned at her. "Are you talking to yourself?"

"Yes—I mean, no," Ali replied, flustered. She glanced nervously at the lamp. The tiniest bit of pink smoke was still drifting around it.

Ali hoped Mary wouldn't notice.

Mary gave her a funny look. "Are you okay?"

"I'm fine," Ali said, trying to look as normal as possible.

"Oh wow, is this the lamp your grandma bought you?" Mary went over to the Lava lamp on the desk and picked it up.

Ali gulped. She hoped Genie wasn't bobbing around with the pink bubbles. "It's cool, isn't it?" she said, her voice high and squeaky.

Grrrrr!

Mary jumped and put the lamp back on the desk. "What was that?" she asked, her eyes wide.

Ali glanced desperately at the sock

drawer. "Oh, it was just my stomach rumbling," she explained quickly. "I didn't have any breakfast. My dad's getting doughnuts."

Grrrrr!

"Wow!" Mary laughed. "You must be *really* hungry, Ali!"

"Starving!" Ali almost shouted. "Come on downstairs. I think I hear Bulldozer. He'll eat all the iced ones if we aren't quick."

Mary nodded. "Have you got all your school stuff ready for tomorrow?" she asked as they traipsed downstairs.

"Not yet," Ali replied, looking back over her shoulder at her room. Was the first day of school really tomorrow? She'd hardly thought about it at all—

she'd had genies and tigers to worry about!

But now Ali had a plan ... a plan for a second wish that would help her put an end to this entire mess!

Chapter Nine
Let's Dance All Night

"Genie!" Ali whispered, tiptoeing into her bedroom at dusk. "Where are you?"

Ali hadn't had a chance to speak to Little Genie all day. After Mary had gone home, Ali and her family had gone over to Gran's for a visit and Sunday dinner, and they'd only just got back.

"Here I am." Little Genie popped her head out of the sock drawer and yawned. Her ponytail was messy.

"I've been crashing with the tiger."

The tiger appeared too, his ears pricked and his black eyes very bright.

"Listen, I've thought of my second wish," Ali said eagerly. "And you're going to like it." She grinned at Little Genie. "I want one hundred chocolate candy bars! That's enough for you and me for at least a week—and I can share them with Mary, too."

Little Genie rubbed her eyes. "Okay. Your wish is my command," she mumbled sleepily. She raised her arms and waved them in the air.

"*Grrr!*" growled the tiger, thinking this was a new game. He jumped up and tried to grab Little Genie's sleeve with his tiny teeth. As he did, his furry tail brushed against Genie's nose.

Little Genie screwed up her face and sneezed loudly. *"Aschoo! Aschoo!"*

There was a flash and then a cloud of purple smoke.

When it cleared, Ali couldn't believe what she was seeing. There were bars of chocolate *everywhere.* They were piled on the bed, spilling onto the floor. They were stacked on the windowsill and on the desk. Ali had never seen so much chocolate in her life!

"Wow!" she cried. "Even more than I was expecting!"

"Oops!" Little Genie looked a bit sheepish. "I must have added two zeros to the hundred when I sneezed. Miss Spelling did say that could happen sometimes. It looks like you've got *ten thousand* chocolate candy bars, Ali!"

Ali grinned. "This is great!" She grabbed one of the bars off the bed and tore open the gold and purple wrapper, her mouth watering. She couldn't wait to dig in.

She took a big bite and stopped.

"What's the matter?" asked Genie.

"This is *dark* chocolate!" Ali groaned, waving the bar at her. "I only like *milk* chocolate." She stared around in despair at the thousands of chocolate bars. "Who's going to eat all these now?"

Little Genie laughed. She climbed out of the drawer, using a sock as a rope ladder, and snapped her fingers to make herself full size. "Don't worry," she said cheerfully, unwrapping one of the bars. "I know someone who loves dark chocolate!" She held the bar out to the tiger, which took it and ate it in two bites, purring loudly.

Ali stared in amazement. "So that's what he eats," she said. "Chocolate!"

"Well, he came from a chocolate ad, didn't he?" Genie replied, unwrapping another bar and eating it herself. She lifted the tiger out of the sock drawer and put him on the floor. He immediately pounced on a bar that had fallen off the bed and started trying to tear the paper off with his sharp teeth. "He likes all kinds."

"I suppose that's where my candy bars went, and all of our cookies too," Ali said.

Little Genie nodded. "I was going to tell you," she said. "One for you," she went on, feeding the tiger another bar of chocolate. "And one for *me*."

"Well, while you two have your feast, I'm going to bed," Ali said a bit grumpily, pulling on her pajamas.

Little Genie didn't seem to hear her. "Another one for you," she said. "And another one for me!"

Ali snuggled down in bed and tried to get to sleep. But it was very difficult. Little Genie kept on rustling the foil chocolate wrappers, and the tiger was purring away like a little engine.

At last the noise stopped. Ali crept out of bed and went to peek into the sock drawer. Little Genie had shrunk back down to lamp size. She and the tiger were curled up together, fast asleep. Empty wrappers surrounded them, and their faces were smeared with chocolate.

Ali got back into bed, feeling very relieved—until the snoring started. It was louder than a train rumbling past the window!

"Genie!" Ali rolled out of bed again and tapped on the sock drawer. "Stop snoring!"

"What?" Genie said in a hurt voice, sitting up. "Genies don't snore! It must be the tiger."

"You're *both* snoring, and you're keeping me awake!" Ali groaned. Then she had an idea. "Hang on, I've still got my third wish. I wish for something to help me sleep!"

Genie thought for a moment, then clapped.

"What have you done?" Ali asked, looking around nervously. She didn't want *this* spell to go wrong!

"Look," said Genie, pointing at Ali's desk.

Ali almost fell over backward. The pictures of the five guys from BoyFrenzy had vanished from her pillow. And now a tiny band was standing on Ali's desk, smiling at her!

"That's B-B-B-BoyFrenzy!" Ali stammered.

Genie beamed. "I brought them to life from your pillow!" she explained. "They're going to sing you to sleep."

"Sing me to sleep?" Ali gasped.

"Yes, so get into bed," Little Genie instructed.

Still feeling a bit dazed, Ali climbed back under the covers. Wait till she told Mary about this! Well, she couldn't *actually* tell Mary, could she? She had promised to keep Little Genie a secret. And anyway, Mary wouldn't believe her in a million years!

"Come on, boys," Little Genie called, waving her hands like a conductor. "One, two, three!"

The band immediately started singing Ali's favorite song, "Let's Dance All Night."

"Hey, this is great!" Little Genie scrambled out of the sock drawer. "Come on, tiger, let's dance!"

Ali couldn't help laughing as Genie began to twist around on the bedside rug, wiggling her hips and making her ponytail spin. She looked like Ali's gran doing her dance moves from the sixties! Meanwhile, the tiger bounced around Genie, waving his tail in time to the music.

"Neato, guys," Genie called to BoyFrenzy when the song was over. "But it's not exactly helping Ali get to sleep. How about something a bit more mellow?"

The band nodded and began singing a slower number, their latest hit. Now Little Genie and the tiger were both yawning as much as Ali. Genie climbed back into the sock drawer and snuggled down into one of Ali's socks.

But the tiger stayed on the floor, too sleepy to move. Ali had to get out of bed, pick him up, and pop him gently into the drawer. Then she snuggled down under the covers, the faces of BoyFrenzy blurring in her mind. Having her very own genie was the best thing ever, she thought as her eyes began to close.

Chapter Ten
Three More Wishes

When Ali woke up the next morning, the first thing she noticed was that the BoyFrenzy pictures were back on her pillow again. She sat up, pushing her hair out of her eyes, and looked around her room. All the chocolate bars had vanished too.

"Genie?" she called in a low voice.

Genie's head popped out of the sock drawer. "The tiger's gone," she said sadly.

Ali glanced down at the magazine on the floor. It was still open to the chocolate advertisement, and the tiger's picture was back on the page.

"Your wishes have finished," Genie added. "Look." She held out her wrist.

All the grains of pink sand had run through to the bottom half of the hourglass. "Oh," Ali said, feeling a bit sad. The tiger had been so cute, and she'd kind of gotten used to having him around. And she'd only just found out what he liked to eat!

"The only thing that's left is the foil from the chocolate bars," Genie went on. She climbed out of the drawer, went over to the bed, and lifted up the sheet. "I put it under here."

Ali swung herself over the edge of the bed and peered underneath. There was a *huge* stack of foil piled up on the floor.

"What are you going to do with it?" asked Genie, climbing up Ali's duvet and perching on her pillow.

"I don't know," Ali replied, pulling out a handful of wrappers. "But I'd better get rid of it before Mom sees it."

At that very moment the door opened and Mrs. Miller came in.

"Too late!" Genie whispered, whisking herself out of sight behind Ali's pillow.

"Ali, time to get up! First day of school," Mrs. Miller began. Then she stopped and stared at the handful of foil Ali was holding. "What on earth is that?"

"Foil?" Ali managed to squeak out.

"I can see that," said her mom, frown- ing. "But what's it from?" Before Ali could stop her, she glanced under the bed. "Goodness me!" She gasped. "There's more of it under here!"

"I could make it disappear," Little Genie whispered in Ali's ear.

"No!" Ali whispered back. She didn't want Genie doing any magic while Mom was in the room!

"Ali, what's going on?" demanded her mom. "Where did all this foil come from?" She sniffed. "And it smells like chocolate."

Ali thought fast. "It's for school," she explained. "We're going to be collect- ing foil to raise money for charity. I— I wanted to get a head start."

"Oh." Mom softened. "That's a very good idea, but we can't store all this foil here. It's an ant's paradise! I'll call the school and ask where we can drop it off."

"No, don't do that," Ali said quickly. "I want it to be a surprise for my teacher. I'll take it to school myself this morning."

"Are you sure?" Her mom looked at her doubtfully. "There's so much of it."

"It'll fit in my new backpack," Ali said, hoping she was right.

While her mom went downstairs to make breakfast, Ali got dressed. Then she and Little Genie stuffed the foil into Ali's backpack. Soon the backpack was bulging. They couldn't fit it all in, so they had to use Ali's new wheeled suitcase too.

"I've hardly got room for any of my new books and pens!" Ali complained.

"I'll help you carry it," Little Genie offered.

Ali stared at her. "You can't come to school with me," she said firmly. "Especially not today." There was always lots going on the first day of school, and Ali knew she wouldn't be able to keep an eye on Little Genie and stop her from getting into trouble.

Genie's ponytail drooped. "Oh. Okay." She glanced out the window, and her face brightened. "I can see Marmalade next door! I'll go and play with him, and make sure none of those mean old cats come back. After all, Mrs. Carter thinks he's really brave now!"

"Good idea," Ali replied, fastening her backpack. "Just stay out of trouble, will you?"

Little Genie made a silly face. "Of course I will!"

"I'll see you tonight," Ali said, groaning as she picked up the heavy backpack. A thought suddenly struck her. "When am I going to get my next three wishes?" she asked. "I could wish for someone strong to carry all this foil to school for me!"

Little Genie clapped a hand to her mouth. "The wishes!" she gasped. "I almost forgot! Ali, come back!"

"What's the matter?" Ali spun around in the doorway.

"We have to prepare for your next

set of wishes," Little Genie said solemnly.

"How?"

"I must turn the hourglass upside down," Little Genie explained. "And when the sand starts to run through, then your next set of wishes will start."

Ali watched excitedly as Little Genie slowly turned the hourglass on her wrist. Now the top half of the hourglass was full of pink sand. But to Ali's disappointment, the sand did not begin to trickle through the hourglass. It stayed right where it was.

"Does that mean I'm not going to get any more wishes?" Ali asked glumly.

Little Genie shook her head. "No, I remember this from Genie School," she said. "Sometimes there's a gap between each set of wishes." She grinned at Ali. "Don't worry. One day the sand will start to run through the hourglass, and you'll have three wishes all over again!"

Ali felt a shiver of excitement at Genie's words. Okay, so maybe all her wishes hadn't worked out *quite* so well this time. But next time she'd think really carefully about what she wanted and try to avoid all the trouble Genie had caused!

"Three more wishes," Ali whispered to herself as she raced downstairs. She could hardly wait!

About the Author

Miranda Jones lives in a regular house in
London. She's sure a genie bottle would
be much more exciting.

Read more about the adventures
of Ali and Little Genie in
Little Genie: *Double Trouble!*

Ali doesn't feel like going to school today.
And with Little Genie around, she doesn't
have to.
She'll let Genie take her place!
Is it a good idea to let a little genie pretend
to be a human girl?
The sparkling pink sand in Little Genie's
watch is starting to move—time for Ali to
make a wish and find out!